THE DAY THAT A RAN AWAY

OTHER BOOKS BY THE SAME AUTHOR:

The Grumpface
Henry and the Hidden Treasure
Titch the Itch
Don't Ever Look Behind Door 32

THE DAY THAT A RAN AWAY

B.C.R. Fegan

Cover art and illustrations by Lenny Wen

The moral right of the author has been asserted.

Published by TaleBlade Press

TaleBlade

www.taleblade.com

For Amelia

THE DAY THAT A RAN AWAY

B.C.R. FEGAN

ILLUSTRATED BY
LENNY WEN

TaleBlade

'Oh no!' said the teacher. 'Master Jet,
You haven't written the alphabet.'

'I did, Mrs May,' said Jet in dismay, 'but...

Today was the day that **A** ran away.'

B was so sad that she didn't stay.

C left as well; he wanted to play.

D's scared of school
and went into hiding.

E followed next.
I think he went riding.

F never made it;
perhaps she got lost.

G wasn't free.
He said that he cost.

H was upset all the letters were going.

I didn't care. He shrugged
and went rowing.

J found it funny and stepped off the page.

K was annoyed and went into a rage.

L just went missing.
I think it was theft.

M would have stayed, but the others had left.

N was hungry and went out to eat.

O rolled away when I lifted the sheet.

P will be back; she only stepped out.

Q isn't far;
he's milling about.

R left and said this book's not her style.

S said she'd join her.
They've been gone a while.

T was just here,
only moments ago.

U didn't come.
Boy was she slow.

V was annoying.
I'm glad that he went.

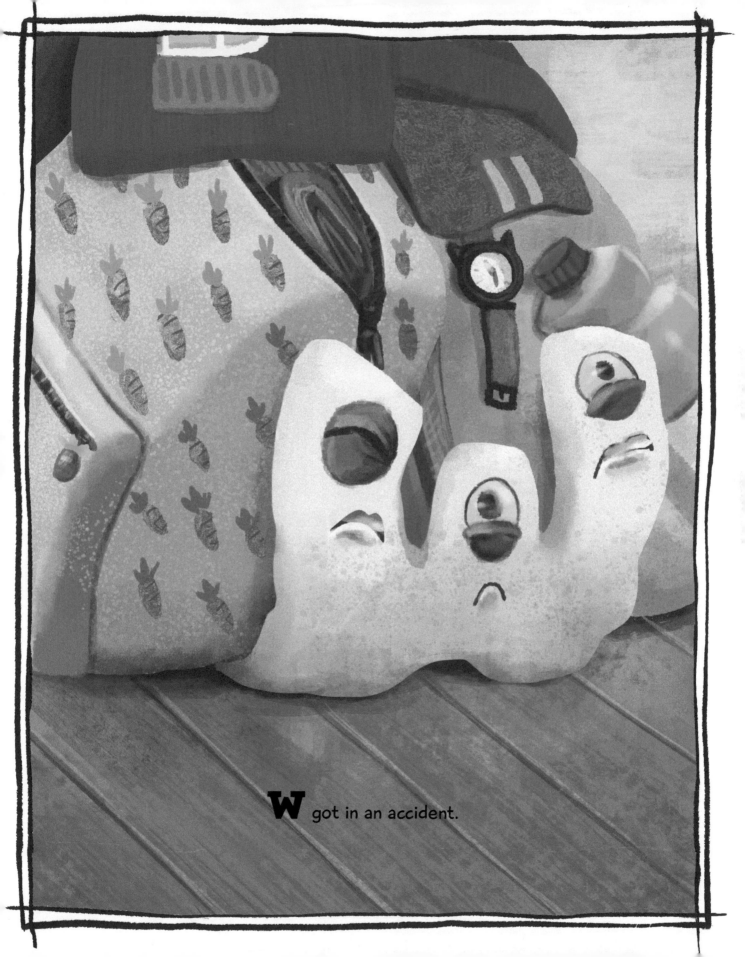

W got in an accident.

X marked a spot — it just wasn't here.

Yoh why did they all disappear?

That leaves us with **Z**,
And I'm sorry to say,
Though I wish he was here,
He too ran away.

Mrs May smiled, 'I see Master Jet
As to why you are missing
your alphabet.

But don't be so sad, they'll
pay for their crimes.
For running away...

Write them down twenty times.'

CPSIA information can be obtained
at www.ICGtesting.com
Printed in the USA
LVHW070023281118
598479LV00008B/40/P

9 781925 810004